"The Story of Blind Beauty"

"ᛒᛚᛁᚾᛞ
ᛒᛖᚢᛏᛁ "

In a royal realm, there lived a newlywed king. He and his wife enjoyed their love, their wedding, and their first new moon together. Upon the royal couple's return to their thrones, a young man appeared before the king's courts requesting an audience with the king. The royal guards and court ministers questioned the man and upon thorough examination let the man into the king's presence. The young man was a prophet or, in olden times, what kings used to call a "Seer."

This prophet or seer was well-known and wise and had the respect of many of the king's loyal subjects. When the king saw him - in his joy, he welcomed him kindly, yet he could see by the look on the man's face that he brought the king a serious and somber message. The king's countenance changed, and, - in his heart, he prepared to hear ill news, yet still, he had hope. The seer said with clear and respectful words, "O King, live forever, but hear now my words, the Creator has declared to me that your kingdom has been cursed and that a great evil has befallen your realm and your lands and yes, even to the womb of your love. Behold your firstborn carried in the Queen's womb shall be a girl of exceeding beauty, and hers shall be unlike any before in the world of men. But though her beauty shall surpass that of even the stars in the sky, she will be born blind, and after her birth, the womb of your wife will be shut. But there is hope, my lord. Hope that the curse of your kingdom will be broken and that your line and your love will endure. The man who chooses to marry your most beautiful daughter will himself become blind, but he will lift the curse. That is what I know, O King, what

I have said, I have said, and I run not from your wrath nor from your tears."

For as the young man spoke, he saw pain, anger, and mournful tears falling from the king's face. Many words and questions and long conversations were had between the king and the young man before the king ordered his arrest. The young man was sentenced to a year in prison, in a great dungeon of the realm. It was done to see if his word was true, but he was not to be ill-treated or tortured.

As spring became summer and summer to winter, the queen's belly grew, and at the turning of the new year, she gave birth to a beautiful baby girl. And as the weeks passed, they saw that she was exceedingly beautiful and completely blind. And love and sorrow grew greatly in the king's heart. The young man was released and given freedom, and though it pained the king, he requested that the seer remain in his city to give the king his council whenever he had need of it. The seer eventually befriended the king and his family and became a respected court attendant.

The years passed, and as the young seer said, the king had no more children. Yet, year after year, his daughter became more and more beautiful.

The king named his daughter ᚠᛖᛁ ᚨ ᚺ -ᛁ ᚨ ᚺᚠᛖ, which sounds like Feyah- Yahfe. Her name meant, "Beauty of the LORD, or the LORD is beautiful."

He and his wife, the queen, cared for their daughter in her blindness and tried to let her live with joy and peace, without letting her inability frustrate them or her. Feyah became not only most beautiful but very wise, and her father, the king, saw that her inability to see actually made his daughter even more lovely. For beauty among women who can see causes jealousy and pride and envy and malice - and yet because his daughter could not see herself, she was spared from many temptations that other women who could see fell victim to. She became humble, obviously needing help herself with many things, but she also became very kind and good at listening and caring for the people she grew to know, including the seer who foretold her birth.

Throughout her youth and teenage years, she learned many crafts, how to work and make things with her hands, and she became an inquisitive listener and learner. She loved gardening, walking, swimming, exercising, singing and making music, relaxing by a fire in the cool of night, and listening to and telling wonderful stories.

Whenever the king held court, the queen and his daughter were summoned, and as she listened, Feyah discerned good and evil - right from wrong. ᚠᛖᛁ ᚨ ᚺ - ᛁ ᚨ ᚺᚠᛖ received wisdom as she learned about; Love, Judgement, Justice, Mercy, Kindness, Generosity, Reconciliation, and Redemption. She was most compassionate toward the poor, for she was moved with loving pity as she heard their stories and would even plead with her father on their behalf to help the people that sounded the most desperate and, at the same time, genuine. And when her father had not the resources, she would help some of them to her own detriment.

Feyah became so good at listening that she could actually hear the tone of sincerity in a person's voice and discern it. She could also hear the difference in the tones of liars and thieves and murderers. She thus learned how to distinguish good and evil in people. And she learned to trust truth and by truth judge the words and tones she heard. Throughout the years, many people from foreign kingdoms came to the courts of the king and when they beheld Princess Feyah-Yahfe, they were truly amazed, - even mystified.

It is amazing to meet a blind person, - seeing someone who cannot see. It humbles you in a way, in a way that my words don't fully explain.

So, when people would see Feya that she was not only blind but most beautiful and wise among women, they began to greatly desire her. Indeed, the story of the blind beauty spread to lands and kingdoms far beyond, but so too did the rumors and knowledge of the curse. The king made the story known to the traveling foreigners that when Feya turned 21, she would be able to become a bride. He had it proclaimed to them and to everyone in his kingdom that he would give his daughter to any man of noble or common birth so long as he was good and willing to become blind, for that is what the seer said would happen to the man who would marry Feya.

Well, the year of her 21st birthday came - and it went…

And many a man came to look upon the blind beauty, but none dared to lose his sight…

In fact, every man of marrying age in the king's kingdom came to behold the princess, and each, when they saw her were amazed and mystified - yet each after looking and seriously considering decided they would rather keep their sight. The king was disheartened, and even Feya's heart felt unwanted. She, like any young virgin, had desire, but she obviously didn't judge a man by his appearance. She was aware of the things unseen, namely the things of one's heart.

Four more years passed, and with each year, there came fewer and fewer visitors or what the kings called "potential suitors." Hope itself almost seemed lost now to the king but not to Feya. She knew in her heart that the Creator gave her life for a reason and that her blindness, to a certain extent, had been a gift to her. She heard much flattery and talk and hearsay about how she looked, but she knew in her heart what that led to, and she purposed to focus on what she could feel, because, well - she was blind, and for a blind person, feeling is very, very important. She didn't allow her heart to become corrupted by her beauty. She was pure-hearted and beautiful inwardly, and outwardly. And that should be enough for any man to marry. But men, many men - are selfish.

Feya learned that the curse of her father's kingdom was that men had become corrupt, greedy, lustful, unloving, and selfish. She knew in her heart that loving someone wholeheartedly was a sacrifice. And thus, she learned that the young men of their kingdom were not willing to love her the way she deserved. And because of that, she wept. But she wept with hope.

Many things I could write and say about the mind of Feya, even more about the heart of Feya, but what remained true of both of them during her time of longsuffering was this - she kept them pure, and therefore, she remained the most beautiful.

In a land far away from her father's kingdom, a young prince heard her story and was, like all other men, fascinated by it. His father, a Vi-king of the north, heard the story from one of his faithful heralds, whom he sent to the courts of Feya's father – to thus behold the blind beauty with his own eyes. The messenger who beheld Feya, like many others, was mystified in wonder of her beauty and of the curse of a once great kingdom.

After a time, the messenger returned north to the halls of his king, and there he informed the Northmen of the mysterious and yet wonderful tragedy. He told them the story of the blind beauty. Upon hearing the tale told in full, the eldest prince of the Northmen asked leave of his liege to seek out and see this blind beauty, and, if God so willed, even to betroth himself to her. The prince's name was Beothain (ᛒ ᛖ ᛟ ᚦ ᚨ ᛁ ᚾ), a young but mighty prince of the far northern realm. He and his loyal brothers set out at the waning of summer to seek the realm of Feya's father.

Over sea and over land they came, traveling through perilous seas and mighty woods. They reached the realm of the blind beauty three and a half months after they set out. As they beheld the land, they imagined with great wonder and anticipation of the beauty of this king's daughter. For the land was also gloriously beautiful in the men's eyes. Up, through a great ring of high mountains they climbed, filled with the scent of tall and ancient pines - and down they went into a peaceful valley filled with gentle streams and flowing rivers, farmers' fields, and hillside cottages, and at the far end of the eastern ring of mountains, there they beheld from a great distance the towers and walls of the king's city, Deorot - in the land of the Pinerhing Mountain. For at that far end of the mountain ring range grew a great and mighty peak. To the Northmen and especially to Beothain, the sight of the peak of Pinerhing mountain looked like a great jewel that shined upon the land, giving majesty.

They camped at the crest of the pass for the night, observing the land and His (God's) beauty. They also beheld a long yet narrow lake in the middle of the great valley; it was many miles before the gates. It looked calm, still, like glass. They also could see the king's highway that seemed to weave its way to the gates of the city in the valley below. The men ate, spoke, and watched the fire and the shining stars. And after their night's rest, they journeyed for three more days taking their time to enjoy the land they beheld before reaching the city gates of Deorot. King Friedriec, the father of Feya, heard the news of the Northmen's coming. He prepared to gather his court at noon of the 4th day of October, which was the day after the Northmen arrived to the gates of Deorot (ᛞᛖᛟᚱᛟᛏ).

Beothain and his followers took council together and found their rest in the king's city. The Northmen were informed by the seer that they would meet with the king in his court on the morrow at noon. That night Beothain prayed in the tongue of his people to the GOD of all earth. What he spoke was deep and powerful, pure and true. And when his words were finished, he listened in silence - still and sure. After a time, Beothain knew in his heart that what he would see would change his life forever.

And so it was, on that morrow at noon, that Beothain and his friends entered the courts of the king and beheld him and his family. As they entered, they bowed their heads with one knee to the ground, and after they arose, Beothain spoke thus, "Hail Friedriec son of Wilhelm, King of Deorot, I am Beothain, son of King Threodor of the far northern realm. These are my loyal companions, Thanes (Thegns), as good as brothers and warriors like myself. We come to seek and to see your daughter ᚠᛖᛁ ᚨ ᚺ-ᛁ ᚨ ᚺᚠᛖ (Feyah-Yahfe), the blind beauty as told by our herald." Then King Friedriec arose from his throne and greeted his guests kindly with a smile and renewed hope in his heart. He gestured with his hand for them to approach, and so they did. To the king's right sat the queen fair like the moon, and to his left sat the princess whose beauty shined like the stars above. When Beothain first saw her, his heart seemed to leap as it beat inside him, and yet he stopped and became as still as stone. Poems of his clan had been sung of women whose beauty was far lesser than that which he now beheld - and in that moment, he knew that he looked upon the fairest face among women that he would ever see.

And he breathed deeply, inhaling glory and exhaling wonder at the sight of the blind beauty.

King Friedriec had seen men's expressions many times before when they looked upon his daughter for the first time, and Beothain's was not unlike the others. At first, he looked sad, even mournful - then, raising his eyebrows, he seemed compassionate with longing and wonder, which then led to a small yet gentle smile that formed on his lips and remained there.

When Feya was informed that Beothain was seeing her, she smiled with her teeth seemingly gleaming, and so smiled Beothain with his teeth showing. It was the most beautiful sight his eyes had ever seen, surpassing the seas, surpassing the trees, mountains, and yes - surpassing even the stars in the sky! Beothain closed his eyes gently and bowed his head softly toward the princess in honored reverence, still smiling with his teeth showing. He then turned to her father and spoke, "I have now looked upon that which is fairest among women. Would you allow me to speak to your daughter, O king of beauty?" The king solemnly nodded and said, "Yes."

The grace with which Beothain spoke to Feyah is comparable to the sound of the cardinal songbird of spring after winter's end. He sounded like a man who longs for love.

"Feyah, the fairest, I have traveled over land and sea to behold thy beauty! And I have thought long and well about what I now say to you. Love to me has been like a rare jewel hidden in the earth. I have not found it, yet I know and believe that it exists. So, my heart has dared to endeavor to find that for which it longs. Even you, O princess daughter!

In my father's kingdom, there are many fair women, blonde and beautiful, but their hearts corrupt, and thus their beauty turns to shame. Sin in their hearts and minds blinds them even as they see. And love among them is altogether forgotten!

Love is pure – it's will waits, and it suffers long for that which it desires to receive.

I have kept myself pure among my people and have not lusted after vain beauty. Yet my heart was made to desire it - beauty, beauty that is pure, beauty that is true…

Hear now my word, O my Love, for though sightless, yet you may see... I have a poem for thee. A revelation of my heart to woo you even unto myself. That you may know me. Respect me. Trust me. And come to love me without fear."

And Beothain said thus,

"What is a lily to the sun?

What is beauty that is seen?

What is the song left unsung?

What is virtue, O my Queen?

Where is wisdom found among women?

And where is she who is rarer than jewels?

Where in her heart is it hidden?

Where sits the Queen who rules?

Why do flowers fade and die?

Why do mothers sing and cry?

Why is LOVE our heart's desire?

And why are we drawn to the glowing fire?

When will you come, O LOVE?
When will you be forever mine?
When sun is dark and moon is dimmed?
When stars refrain to shine?
Who is this whom my soul loves?
And who is she that I see?
Who can have all of LOVE?
Who is this, can it be?"

As Beothain spoke, two tears gently fell down along both sides of the fair face of Feyah, for in her heart, she heard the voice of the LOVE she had so longed for, that she had hoped for. And as he finished speaking, he gazed intently at the glistening tear lines and listened.

Feyah said, "My heart has ached. My heart has longed. My heart has waited to hear your precious words, my lord and my LOVE, and I receive them with tears of joy."

And Beothain thought, "Sometimes tears are worth more than thousands of words."

And he closed his eyes, smiled and bowed his head yet again to the princess. "Feyah," he said softly, "I do betroth myself unto you now this day, but grant that I may look upon you for one year before we wed, that I may enjoy my sight of you - that we may talk and walk together in love before my sight is gone - and what must be will be."

She smiled again, and so began the love and courtship of Feyah-Yahfe and Beothain.

As they parted that day, Beothain sang a song to the princess, and as he did, his men hummed a patterned chant of an ancient Norse hymn. The sound was deep, like the sea waves reaching the rocks of the shore, yet kind, like the happy song of birds in springtime.

"She shines like the sun,

Bright as the Moon,

Beautiful like stars in the sky.

She fair as the day, yet mysterious like the night -

still giving her light.

She - more awesome than ships on the high sea - sailing with banners!"

He sang slow and softly with deep power and reverence, and free exhales.

The year came and went, and with each passing day, their love grew purer and stronger.

Beothain learned what life was like for his blind beloved. But in her beauty, he saw his destiny and faced his future without fear - for he knew that his love was true and sure, and in that, he felt peace.

The month of their union came, and with it, great jubilation and wondrous mystery. For no one knew what the lifting of the curse would mean for their kingdom or, for that matter, how soon after they wed that their new prince would become blind.

The two of them had many conversations about how they would care for one another after their marriage. They talked about faithfulness, children, leadership, God, LOVE, submission, protecting trust, forgiveness, peace, maintaining purity, keeping faith, grace, rule, order, work, discipline, child rearing, dreams, goals, food, friendship, fun, fellowship, finances, cleaning, humor, romance, traveling, respecting one another, humility, service, legacy and so many other things - not least of all what it meant for each of them to sacrifice for one another.

Obviously, Beothain was making a huge sacrifice to marry ᚠᛖᛁ ᚨ ᚺ-ᛁ ᚨ ᚺᚠᛖ, but it was a sacrifice that he believed was worth it. His loss was also one of his greatest gains. However, not all things in the future are foreseen by men. They knew their love would be tested and tempted, but they did not know in what ways.

From the north hearkened thirty ships filled with Beothain's kinsman, a mighty throng of people set sail to celebrate and honor the Love and sacrifice of their worthy lord. Among that host was King Threodor, who brought with him gold in abundance and mead for merriment to thus bless his beloved son’s union. He also gave to his son a rare ring fashioned for the hand of Feyah-Yahfe. It was made in homage of his lineage, in the beauty and style of ancient northern chieftains who gave rings to their loyal lovers – the maidens of old.

Feyah’s family gathered as well, and King Friedriec proclaimed that all in his kingdom be summoned to Deorot the week preceding the day of their marriage. He further ordered that a great festival of feasting, games, dancing, drinking, and music-making be held during that whole week. The people came in droves – thousands upon thousands, yes - tens of thousands from all over the country. And no greater party was had prior or hence in ᛞᛖᛟᚱᛟᛏ (Deorot)!

At last, the destined day dawned – the wedding of Wyrd, as some men have called it. The ceremony was glorious. Feyah was clothed with white, bright and pure. Beothain wore white as well - he looked handsomely mighty as he beheld the face of his beloved. The seer himself presided at their wedding, which made Feyah especially glad, for he was a very dear friend to her. Sacred words were said, tears were shed, and the rings were given. They kissed - GOD (LOVE) was seen. God was honored. And the final celebration began with the roaring of a jubilant crowd! They walked, danced, ate and drank, told stories, heard stories, laughed with friends, took in the sunset in all its shining glory, felt its warmth, and hugged their parents as well as their friends. They sang songs of praise, listened to music, and held each other's hands. They were married on the high hill overlooking the walls before the valley of Deorot. On that hill was a great stone courtyard surrounded by a wonderful pine tree garden with fountains and streams, fish pools and flowers.

After all the festivities of the celebration settled, Beothain took Feyah in his arms and carried her to the great tower on the crest of that beautiful hill overlooking the whole city of Deorot as well as the whole bowl of mountains making up the Pinerhing Mountain range. And there in that tower on that day, the two became One. And when they were One, a miracle happened...! Feyah's eyes welled with loving tears, and when they fell from her face - she could SEE! When Beothain breathed gently toward her face, he wiped away her tears and smiled and welcomed her new sense with great joy.

She was in awe. He – Beothain, did not expect that his wife would see. And he did not know how long his sight would last.

Neither of them longed for sleep that night, but instead, they held each other close and gazed, it seemed, ever more deeply into each other's eyes!

With the joy of sight came many new delights for Feyah, but Beothain warned her of many great evils and temptations to come. He was the first person she saw, and he, to her, was like a mirror - which reflects glory. Eventually, Beothain showed Feya a mirror, and she beheld herself for the first time. Her identity all her life was focused inwardly toward her heart, but now for the first time, she knew sin and beauty in a different way. She now knew the temptation of pride that she had previously, to a great extent, been spared from. The lust of the eyes that so easily leads hearts astray from LOVE, was now felt in her heart.

But there on that night, though change was sudden and miraculous, and the future implications of that change were being carefully considered and thought out - they decided to be thankful to God and to focus themselves on that which is pure. And so, they did, and thus their joy was fulfilled.

Now, when night lengthened and sleep set in-to his most beautiful wife, Beothain watched her and comforted her as she slept - so peacefully. He watched her breathe in and out with a loving gaze. And as he tired, he fought the sleep, for he knew in his heart what was destined to be. And when he couldn't fight it any more, he leaned over, kissed his wife's forehead ever so gently, then rested his head near hers - he closed his eyes and fell asleep, asleep - and in LOVE.

As morning dawned, he awoke to darkness. He was blind, blind and in LOVE.

And there, for now, is thee END of my tale.

But what remains? Many questions... So many questions...

How should this story end? -Happily ever after? -Faithfully? -With both couples seeing?

What is the price of sight...? What is sight worth? What does it mean to see? How can joy be fulfilled when temptation threatens its existence? Where does beauty come from, and why does it exist? What is beauty's relationship to purity? What is love's relationship to vulnerability?

What is a rock to the waves of the sea?

Who wins the fight - pride vs. humility?

Are there rocks that cannot be broken?

Is love really stronger than death...? (Yes.)

What is the difference between the fire that destroys and the fire that gives life? When will faith become sight? What is seeing your Lover really worth? Where can a man and a woman find security in LOVE? How can they find security in LOVE? Why does Love get tested, tempted, and tried?

GOD's image is BEAUTIFUL, but why does it get tested? Why does God allow His beautiful IMAGE to be broken? Can something be broken and then built back stronger and more beautiful than before? Think about Jesus - The Cross and His Bride. May the Holy Spirit give you insight, comfort, and hope through this story, AMEN! And remember, even when we are unfaithful, God remains faithful…!

Grace and peace to you in Jesus Christ, your brother in the LORD – Alexander James Wiese (ᚨ ᛚ ᛖᚲ ᛊ ᚨ ᚾ ᛞᛖᚱ ᛃ ᚨ ᛗᛖᛊ ᚹᛁ ᛖᛊ ᛖ).

Furthark – 'The Viking Alphabet'

A	ᚨ	I	ᛁ	Q no q	(ᚲ ᚹ)
B	ᛒ	J	ᛃ	R	ᚱ
C no c	(ᚲ or ᛊ)	K	ᚲ	S	ᛊ
D	ᛞ	L	ᛚ	T	ᛏ
E	ᛖ	M	ᛗ	U	ᚢ
F	ᚠ	N	ᚾ	V	ᚹ
G	ᚷ	O	ᛟ	W	ᚹ
H	ᚺ	P	ᛈ	X no x	(ᛖᚲ ᛊ)
	Y	ᛁ	Z	ᛉ	

Thank you all so much for your support. If you want to learn more about Vikings and their history and their culture, I suggest that you explore it for yourselves. Read books, watch videos and movies and documentaries on YouTube, or rentable videos at your local library. I love the movie "The Thirteenth Warrior" with Antonio Banderas, I think it is one of the most historically accurate movies out there regarding Viking culture and it is an awesome adventure story! Or you can even plan a vacation up here to the great state of Minnesota - the Land of 10,000 Lakes and the place where many descendants of the ancient Viking peoples call home, for now. We even have a super cool exhibit up in Alexandria Minnesota where the local legend is - a band of Viking explorers carved their story in stone in the very alphabet that I have given in this book. I have taken a lot of time to learn about their culture and ways over the last 5 years and have found great enjoyment and delight in learning about them. I hope you do too.

I am currently doing a Youtube Podcast on the whole story of Beowulf, a real Viking Thane saga. You are welcome to join me on that adventure @AmericanPreacher07 which is my Youtube Channel name.

I think it is fitting to end this book with two prayers; one the LORD's - and the other the Vikings prayer, which I see now as one of their descendants as an honorable tribute to faith in Jesus Christ and our true Father in Heaven.

"Our Father in Heaven, hallowed be Thy name; Thy Kingdom come; Thy will be done; here on earth as it is in heaven, give us this day our daily bread and forgive us our sins as we are forgiving those who have sinned against us. And lead us not into temptation; but deliver us from the Evil one. For Thine is the Kingdom, and the power, and the GLORY, forever and ever. Amen."

"Lo, there do I see my Father.

Lo, there do I see my mother and my sisters and my brothers.

Lo, there do I see the line of my people, back to the beginning.

Lo, they do call to me, they bid me take my place among them, in the halls of Valhalla - where the brave may live forever!"

Peace...

Made in the USA
Columbia, SC
14 December 2024

49027145R00018